March 2022.

Dearest Reader –

Always be 'shore' of yourself!

With love,

Sea Angel Jenn

A Mermaid's Tale of Pearls

ISBN: 978-1-66781-845-0

I originally wrote this story in high school for a creative writing project. It was dedicated to two of my best friends at the time.

Within a year, I broke one's heart while the other one broke mine. This was originally dedicated to both of them, and for myself to heal.

Today, I dedicate this to my daughter, Aurora Joy, and my niece Olivia Kathleen....and for all the young ones I have been blessed to cross paths with as a baby-sitter, a godmother, a mermaid, a 2nd mom (aka Mama Jenn) and a kids/ youth volunteer.

This book is also for those that have had their hearts broken, have broken a heart, and for those yet to experience both.

Always move forward with kindness. Remember the love that once was there.

—Jennifer Elizabeth

One spring day, a young girl was playing in the ocean tide pools. As she was gathering oyster shells in her bucket, she came upon a beautiful lady with a colorful fish tail.

"Hello," said the lovely Mermaid with a smile. "I was curious what you are doing with that bucket?"

The little girl's eyes widened as she answered, "I am looking for pearls and buried treasure to share with my best friend. Do you know where I could find some treasure, Mermaid?"

The Mermaid laughed lightly, as she took a shell out of the girl's hand and replied, "Sweet Child, let me tell you a real treasure of a tale about pearls. It begins with the love and friendship between the Moon and the deep blue Sea."

The little girl, knowing that just coming across a mermaid was a treasure in itself, quickly sat herself on a rock across from the Mermaid as she began her story....

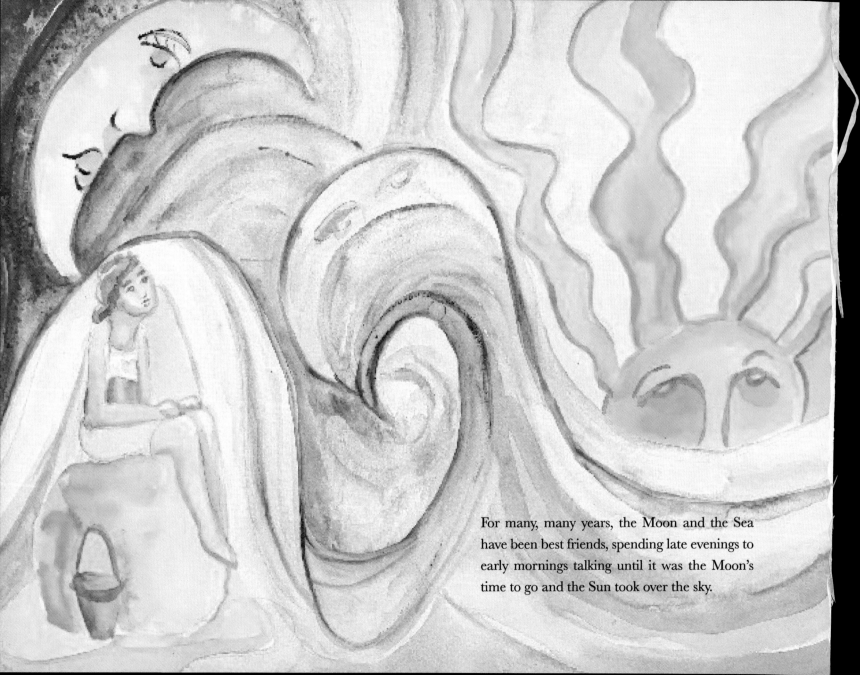

For many, many years, the Moon and the Sea have been best friends, spending late evenings to early mornings talking until it was the Moon's time to go and the Sun took over the sky.

Over the years, as the friendship deepened between the Moon and the Sea, so did the love the Sea had for the Moon.

He was always sad and forlorn on the nights when the Moon was not out.

But my, it was something amazing for the Sea to watch the sliver of the Moon slowly grow to a crescent Moon, then a half a Moon, until finally the Moon was so full and bright, lighting up the whole night sky like one big jewel, that she put the twinkling lights of the stars to shame.

The Moon's light would dance on the Sea's gentle waves and ripples, displaying its true enchantment.

While the Sea would instruct its finest Ocean creatures—the Dolphins and Mermaids - to jump and sing for the moon in her beautiful spotlight.

One day as the Sun was out shining the Earth and warming the top of the Ocean, the Sea decided it was time to express his love to the Moon.

But he didn't know how, or even when…

The Sea waited until the night of the Harvest Moon.

The Sea said to the Moon, "Dear sweet Moon, I wish I could be a Star in the night sky shining beside you. I... care for you dearly."

The Sea had failed to express his whole heart and true feelings... for he really wanted to say, "I love you" to the Moon.

The Moon smiled down at the Sea and said, "Don't feel like you need to be up here with me, Sea. I like you just where you are. I see my reflection upon you, and I can also watch over you. I care for you dearly, too.
You are my best friend."

As a sweet gesture of friendship, the Moon then took the shiniest stars out of the Heavens, and scattered them in the Sea's oceans.

"Now we both have stars to hold and wishes to make come true," replied the Moon. The kind gesture touched the Sea's soul greatly, however, he was not satisfied.

He still needed to tell the Moon how he really loved her. For the Sea's only wish he cared to make come true was that the Moon loved him as much as he loved her.

Nights continued to go by as the Moon and the Sea's friendship deepened.

The Moon talked about a special night coming up for her called the Eclipse, while the Sea's love for the Moon was growing more and more.

It was the night of the Blue Moon when the Sea felt most confident and finally ready to express his love to the Moon.

As the Sun began to descend in the West, and the baby blue sky turned into a deep dark purple, the Moon came out shining bright with just a hint of blue around her.

The Sea tried lifting his waves as high as he could so he could touch the Moon but he could not reach her.

The Moon looked down and smiled, "Good evening, my dear Sea. Do you have something important to say? Your waves are so close to me."

The Sea was silent for a few moments, and then answered, "Yes, I do have something very important to say to you, Moon."

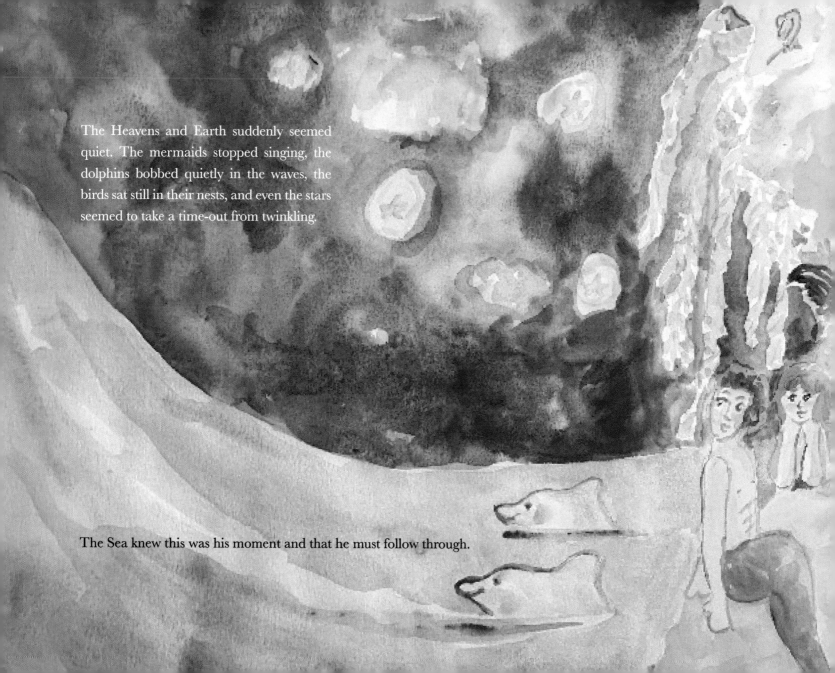

The Heavens and Earth suddenly seemed quiet. The mermaids stopped singing, the dolphins bobbed quietly in the waves, the birds sat still in their nests, and even the stars seemed to take a time-out from twinkling.

The Sea knew this was his moment and that he must follow through.

"My sweet Moon," began the Sea, "you have been a wonderful best friend and I will always be thankful for that and care for you, but I am also in love with you—more than just a friend."

"I love you, Moon."

The Moon was quiet and had tears in her eyes.

"My dear Sea," she replied, "I will always care and love you but only as my best friend and I hope you always will be. My love belongs to my soulmate and my betrothed, the Sun. Our wedding, the great Eclipse, is in just a few nights."

The heartbroken Sea sadly asked, "The Sun? What has the Sun provided for you? I've never seen you with the Sun!"

The Moon replied, "If it wasn't for the Sun's lovely light, you would never see me at night, or our children the stars. I would be invisible, lost and cold in the dark sky."

The Sea silently rocked his waves back and forth trying to shake off the hurt and sadness he felt in the depths of his soul.

The Moon, sensing her best friend's heartache soothingly replied, "My dear sweet Sea, you have given me one of the greatest gifts - Friendship! Even though I can't be with you, Sea," continued the Moon, "I will always be a part of you."

Then the Moon sprinkled a handful of her Moon dust into the shells at the bottom of the Sea. Even though the gift touched the Sea's heart deeply, he did not understand what the Moon meant by "I will always be a part of you."

The Sea's curiosity was quickly answered when the clams opened their shells widely to display a thousand little Moons hidden inside. The Sea was amazed by their smooth and delicate beauty. The Moon replied, "They are the jewels of pure love and friendship. Simple, solid, classic, and timelessly beautiful. They will be called Pearls."

The Sea swayed its waves in agreement and still in awe of the pure beauty of the precious pearls. Then he asked, "Moon, why do only some of the shells have pearls?"

The Moon answered, "Because pure love and friendship is a gift that not everyone is born with. Some need to give it in able to receive it, some need to earn it, and others, never come across it at all."

The Sea, although still heartbroken, was honored with this offering the Moon provided.

On the day of the Eclipse, the Sea looked up at the sky with a bittersweet smile because he saw how truly happy his love, the Moon, was with the mighty Sun... and the Sea held the Moon's gift deep in his heart proudly.

As the Mermaid finished her story, she cracked open the oyster shell from the little girl's hand.
Inside was a beautiful Pearl!

While taking another Pearl off her own necklace the Mermaid said, "Now you have two treasures. These Pearls and a story to share with your best friend."

The enchanting Mermaid then smiled and dove back into the ocean. As the little girl held the pearls close to her heart, she heard the whisper of the Sea and saw the crescent Moon smiling down upon her.

The End.

Jennifer Elizabeth (aka Sea Angel Jenn) has been a professional mermaid for over 10 years, but a mermaid in her heart since she was 5 years old. She performs and makes mermaid appearances around the Los Angeles area and in her hometown, Carmel, CA.

Jenn loves bringing mermaid magic wherever she goes. Writing has always been her secret passion and after writing this story over 20 years ago, is happy to bring it to life to share with all.

Using her mermaid talents scored a small role in an episode of Nickelodeon's 'Knight Squad' as a hologram mermaid fighting a wizard, and she was cast as the Mermaid in a short film (soon to be a feature) titled 'Mermaid'. She has appeared in industrial commercials and music videos with her numerous collection of tails. Jennifer continues to write in many avenues and has few more projects in motion.